ARF AND the THREE DOGS

by Philip Wooderson

ILLUSTRATED BY BRIDGET MACKEITH
COLORS BY JESSICA FUCHS

Librarian Reviewer
Laurie K. Holland
Media Specialist (National Board Certified), Edina, MN
MA in Elementary Education, Minnesota State University, Mankato, MN

Reading Consultant
Sherry Klehr
Elementary/Middle School Educator, Edina Public Schools, MN
MA in Education, University of Minnesota, MN

STONE ARCH BOOKS
Minneapolis   San Diego

First published in the United States in 2006
by Stone Arch Books,
151 Good Counsel Drive, P.O. Box 669,
Mankato, Minnesota 56002.
www.stonearchbooks.com

Originally published in Great Britain in 2003
by A & C Black Publishers Ltd,
38 Soho Square, London, W1D 3HB.

Text copyright © 2002 Philip Wooderson
Illustrations copyright© 2002 Bridget MacKeith

Library of Congress Cataloging-in-Publication Data
Wooderson, Philip.
    Arf and the Three Dogs / by Philip Wooderson; illustrated by Bridget
MacKeith.
       p. cm. — (Graphic Trax)
       ISBN-13: 978-1-59889-021-1 (hardcover)
       ISBN-10: 1-59889-021-2 (hardcover)
       ISBN-13: 978-1-59889-177-5 (paperback)
       ISBN-10: 1-59889-177-4 (paperback)
       1. Graphic novels. I. MacKeith, Bridget. II. Title. III. Series.
PN6727.W66A76 2006
741.5—dc22   2005026689

Summary: Arf decides to use his mother's camera to make money as a reporter and
photographer. When he takes pictures of the neighborhood dogs, Arf realizes that
something strange is happening at the animal shelter.

1 2 3 4 5 6 11 10 09 08 07 06

Printed in the United States of America.

TABLE OF CONTENTS

CAST OF CHARACTERS

MOM

ARF'S SISTERS
(BEE & GLORIA)

ARF

THE THREE
DOGS

MR. SANJAY

MAJOR NIMBY

CRAZY BARNEY

ARF'S DOG
(HOPPA)

CHAPTER ONE

It was Saturday morning.

I'm bored.

Then, Arf, take Hoppa for a walk and pick up a newspaper.

How much will you pay me?

"Mom doesn't have to pay you, Arf. You didn't pay her for your breakfast," said Gloria. She was Arf's older sister.

She's not trying to save up like I am.

As Arf went into the store, he was almost knocked off his feet by two big dogs. They were dragging along an old man . . .

. . . and a little dog behind them.

Watch where you're going!

9

The store manager helped Arf rebuild the stack of baked beans.

Crazy Barney loves his dogs.

Arf picked up a tattered envelope and turned it over.

I think he must have dropped this.

12 cans
Pedigree Chomps
Doggy choc drops
Coffee
Cheese
Toilet paper

Arf hurried out of the store. He looked left and right. Then left again. There was no sign of Barney.

CHAPTER TWO

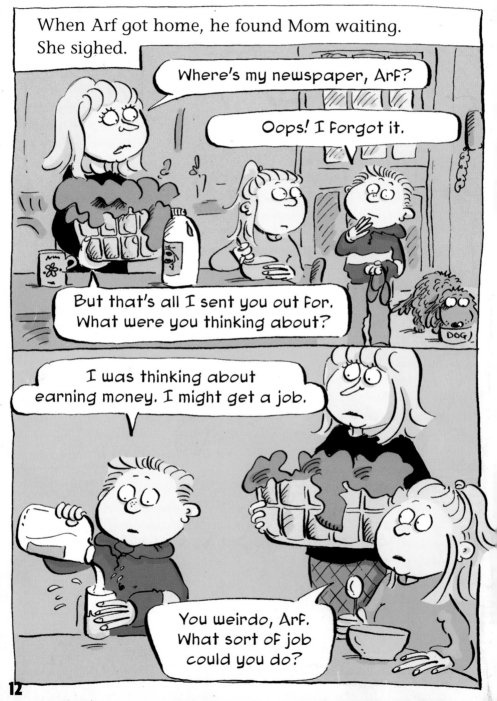

When Arf got home, he found Mom waiting. She sighed.

Where's my newspaper, Arf?

Oops! I forgot it.

But that's all I sent you out for. What were you thinking about?

I was thinking about earning money. I might get a job.

You weirdo, Arf. What sort of job could you do?

15

Mr. Sanjay lived in apartment 3. He worked for the local paper.

You'll have to wait a long time, Arf. Nothing much happens around here.

But then, as if by magic, Arf looked out the window and saw the old man with his two big dogs and . . .

WOOF.

19

But Arf walked up and down the streets for more than half an hour without finding Crazy Barney.

He was ready to give up when he stopped by the animal shelter.

Wow, what a mess.

But as he was walking away . . .

BARK

SCREAM

BARK

What's going on in there?

As Arf got out the camera, the door burst open . . .

WOOF

BARK

. . . and two big dogs bounded out, dragging Crazy Barney behind them, with the little dog close on his heels.

Arf managed to snap three pictures before he was knocked off his feet by the dogs.

23

The man handed Arf his card.

MAJOR NIMBY
CHAIRMAN OF THE RESIDENTS' ACTION GROUP

You're a brave boy, though.

Major Nimby slapped Arf on the back.

Well done, snapping those pictures. I've only gotten shots of the rats infesting this place.

The shelter is a mess. I believe you.

We should help each other.

Arf didn't quite understand this.

Why, what should we do?

You get your photos developed, as fast as you can. Then bring them to me at the town hall. I'll be there at 5:30.

Arf was puzzled.

What for?

The man looked at Arf shrewdly.

I'll pay you $25.

When Arf got back home, there was no one else there. So Arf watched TV and ate three bags of chips . . .

. . . then Mom came home.

Before Arf could explain, there was a knock on the door.

Phew!

!

Hello, Mr. Sanjay.

Arf opened his mouth. But then, through the living room window, he saw his sisters coming home from their Saturday jobs.

He waited for them to walk in and then grinned at his older sister.

I was just telling Mr. Sanjay about the wild dogs at your pet place!

That's nothing to smile about, Arf.

Pet place? You mean the shelter?

39

For the stray pets!

And our Saturday jobs!

Mr. Sanjay turned to Arf.

Now do you understand why Nimby wants these photos?

Can't you take nice photos?

We can find the old man and bring him along to the meeting!

We never found out where he lives, Mom. We don't even know his name.

Then Arf remembered something. Feeling around in his pocket, he brought out the envelope with Barney's shopping list on the back. He turned it over.

CHAPTER FIVE

Mr. Sanjay pressed the buzzer at Barney's apartment. Once they were inside, they walked down the hallway to apartment number 12, Barney Nokes. Barney opened the door. He looked sad.

Mr. Sanjay came straight to the point.

We're wondering if you would come to our protest meeting to try to save the animal shelter?

Arf looked through his photos, only to drop the envelope containing the lottery ticket.

The little dog tried to eat it.

But Arf snatched it away just in time.

He put it down on the table, next to the newspaper, and then he showed Barney the pictures.

The ECHO
PET SHELTER THREATENED

My dogs get angry when I'm angry.

47

Now Barney looked really angry.

The big dogs looked angry.

The little dog looked even angrier.

You don't know this man, do you, Barney?

I worked for him once. Nimby's a crook.

I found out that he was putting mice into the mail slot of a lady's house. He wanted her to move out, so he could knock her house down and build an apartment building.

CHAPTER SIX

It took longer to develop Arf's film than Mr. Sanjay expected. There was lots of traffic, too.

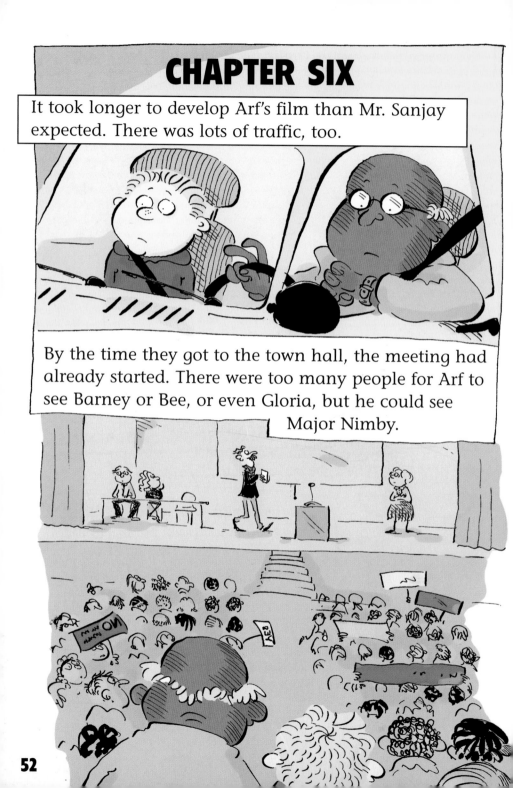

By the time they got to the town hall, the meeting had already started. There were too many people for Arf to see Barney or Bee, or even Gloria, but he could see Major Nimby.

S-m-o-o-t-h

Oh, that's his name. There he is now.

The major pointed at Barney.

Mr. Sanjay pushed Arf forward.

You can't control them. Admit it!

Now is our moment. Quickly!

Arf tried to reach the stage, but people got in the way. He stepped on somebody's toe. This made such a disturbance that Major Nimby noticed.

Ah, here's the innocent victim. Clear the way for him.

Arf found himself being lifted by Major Nimby's friends onto the stage beside him.

Did you bring the pictures?

Arf pulled out some photographs, but they were the ones showing fierce, angry dogs. He put them down on the table, so he could search for the right ones.

While he was trying to find them, the major grabbed the first photos and gave them to his assistant.

She thrust them one by one onto the projector.

Oh, Arf, how could you have done that?

When Arf looked up at the screen, he wished he could disappear. But then, through the silence, he heard Barney call out.

Hey, Major, what are you doing up there in the top left of the picture if you were beating off my dogs?

Arf looked up again at the screen. And yes, there was no doubt about it. The major was emptying a bag over the fence.

What's he up to?

Arf got it.

He's feeding his rats!

That's why the place is infested!

Rats?

Cheater!

Nimby's a fraud!

The meeting ended in an uproar.

CHAPTER SEVEN

Next Saturday, Arf went to the store to pick up the newspaper.

Back home, he opened the front door and was practically knocked off his feet by Barney's two big dogs with their big tongues, trying to lick his face, and . . .

. . . the little dog, too.

Behind him was Mr. Sanjay and Mrs. Hartlepool, who ran the animal shelter.

In the kitchen, there was a cake on the table and a present wrapped in striped paper.

Mr. Sanjay held up his copy of the newspaper, so Arf could read the headline.

Underneath was Arf's photo showing Nimby slyly emptying a bag over the fence.

The caption read, "Crooked builder exposed!"

Congratulations!

Good job, Arf!

64

ABOUT THE AUTHOR

Philip Wooderson has written more than twenty books
for children, including the new young adult suspense
novel, *The Plague, My Side of the Story*. Wooderson lives
in England.

ABOUT THE ILLUSTRATOR

Bridget MacKeith says that being an illustrator is the
only thing she has ever wanted to be. Although she
once thought of being an opera singer! MacKeith's
artwork appears in dozens of children's books.
She currently lives in a small town in the middle of the
Salisbury Plain in England, with her husband, Gareth,
her two children, and a big, hairy Newfoundland
dog named Rudi. She also illustrates "a lot of cards
for Hallmark."

GLOSSARY

develop (di-VEL-uhp)—to treat camera film with chemicals in order to produce pictures

disease (duh-ZEEZ)—an illness

disturbance (di-STUR-buhnss)—something that bothers people

expose (ek-SPOZE)—to reveal the truth about someone or something

infested (in-FESS-tid)—full of unwanted things, such as animals or germs

innocent (IN-uh-suhnt)—not guilty

lottery (LOT-ur-ee)—a game people play for the chance to win a prize

menace (MEN-iss)—a threat to people

protest (PROH-test)—to state your beliefs against something in public

uproar (UP-ror)—noise and shouting

victim (VIK-tuhm)—a person who is tricked or treated unfairly

villain (VIL-uhn)—a bad or evil person

INTERNET SITES

Do you want to know more about subjects related to this book? Or are you interested in learning about other topics? Then check out FactHound, a fun, easy way to find Internet sites.

Our investigative staff has already sniffed out great sites for you!

Here's how to use FactHound:

1. Visit *www.facthound.com*

2. Select your grade level.

3. To learn more about subjects related to this book, type in the book's ISBN number: **1598890212**.

4. Click the **Fetch It** button.

FactHound will fetch the best Internet sites for you.

DISCUSSION QUESTIONS

1. Why does Arf believe Major Nimby's story about the rats?

2. Arf tries to take photographs to make money, but at the end of the story, he decides to walk dogs to earn money. Do you have chores that you do to make money? What are they?

3. Why does Major Nimby like Arf's photographs of the dogs?

WRITING PROMPTS

1. Sometimes the truth is difficult to see, such as when Arf believed the bad things Major Nimby told him about the animal shelter. Have you ever been fooled by someone who wasn't being honest? Write what that person told you. How did it make you feel?

2. Barney loves his three dogs. Describe your pet or a pet you wish you had.

3. There are two sides to every story. Imagine you are a newspaper reporter who saw a dog running loose in your neighborhood. First, write a story that makes people think the dog is causing problems. Second, write a story that makes people feel sorry for the dog.

ALSO BY
PHILIP WOODERSON

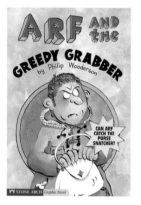

Arf and the Greedy Grabber

Arf loves practical jokes. His tricks give him and his sisters a laugh . . . until a real thief turns up.

Arf and the Metal Detector

Arf can't help himself. When a package for his neighbor shows up at his house, Arf has to see what's inside. The package leads him to more trouble, a couple of crooks, and a buried treasure.